Let's Draw!

First published by Parragon in 2012

Parragon
Chartist House
15-17 Trim Street
Bath BA1 1HA, UK
www.parragon.com

Designed by Talking Design
Illustrations by Carol Seatory
Written by Frances Prior-Reeves

ISBN 978-1-4454-7240-9
Printed in China

Let's Draw!

PaRragon

Bath · New York · Singapore · Hong Kong · Cologne · Delhi
Melbourne · Amsterdam · Johannesburg · Auckland · Shenzhen

Draw the other half of this
robot.

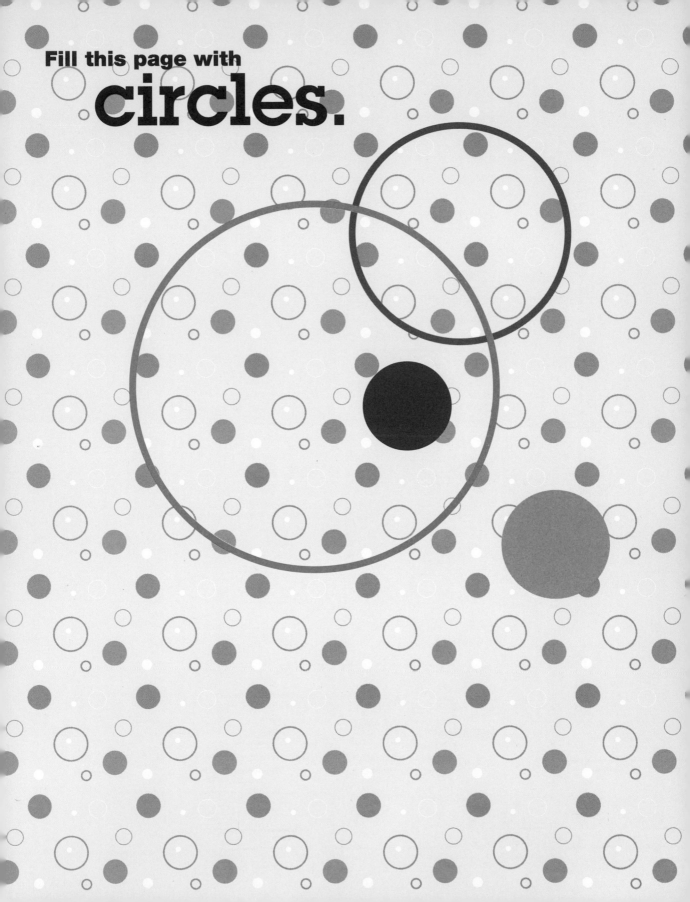

Fill this page with
circles.

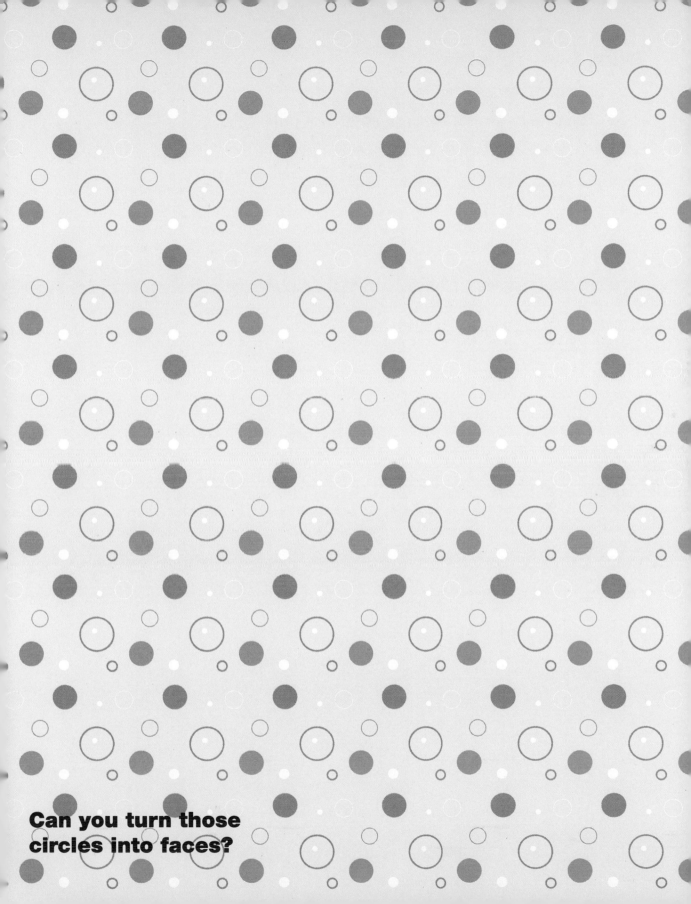

Can you turn those circles into faces?

Draw your favorite

mythical creature.

Boom

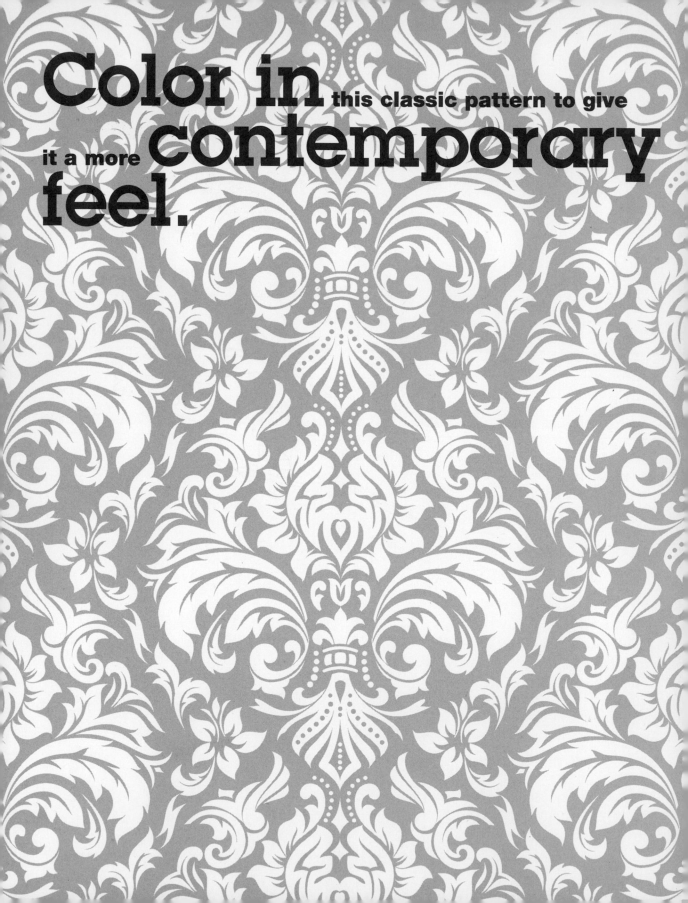

Color in this classic pattern to give it a more contemporary feel.

Your creative space.

Add your own design to this

vase.

Design a flower pot in any shape and then add your own detail.

Fill these shelves.

Fill these pages with bright and colorful
monsters <small>to play with.</small>

Fill this page with

squares.

Can you turn those squares into
robots and
machines?

Fill these pages with beautiful
butterflies.

Draw half of **your** face on one side of the circle and draw half of a **monkey's** face on the other side.

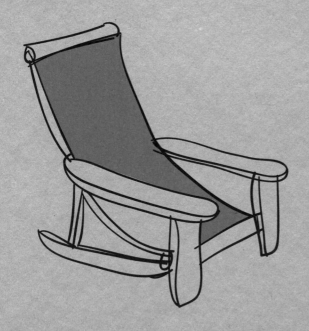

Draw, shade, doodle, and color anything.

Add color, texture, and patterns to this spiral.

Draw the other half of this train.

Design these fabulous tiles
so that each one is unique.

Draw a rocket

flying to the moon.

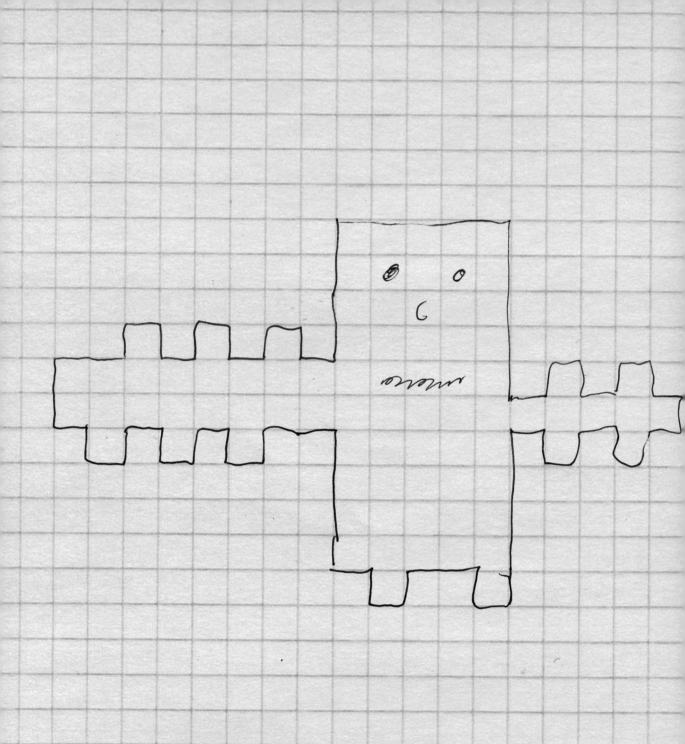

Use the **gridlines**
to guide your doodles.

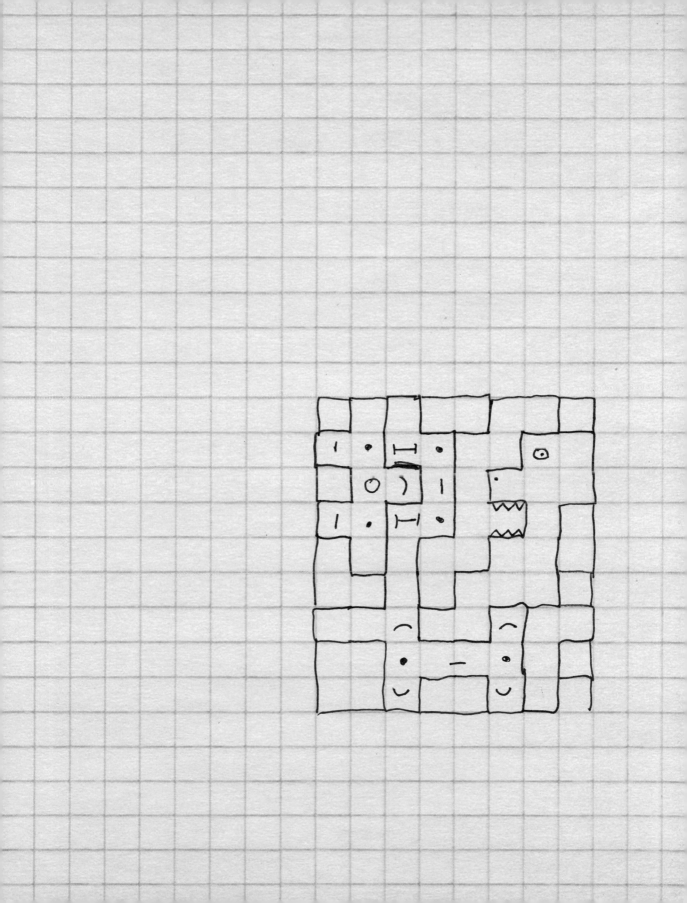

Fill this room with furniture.

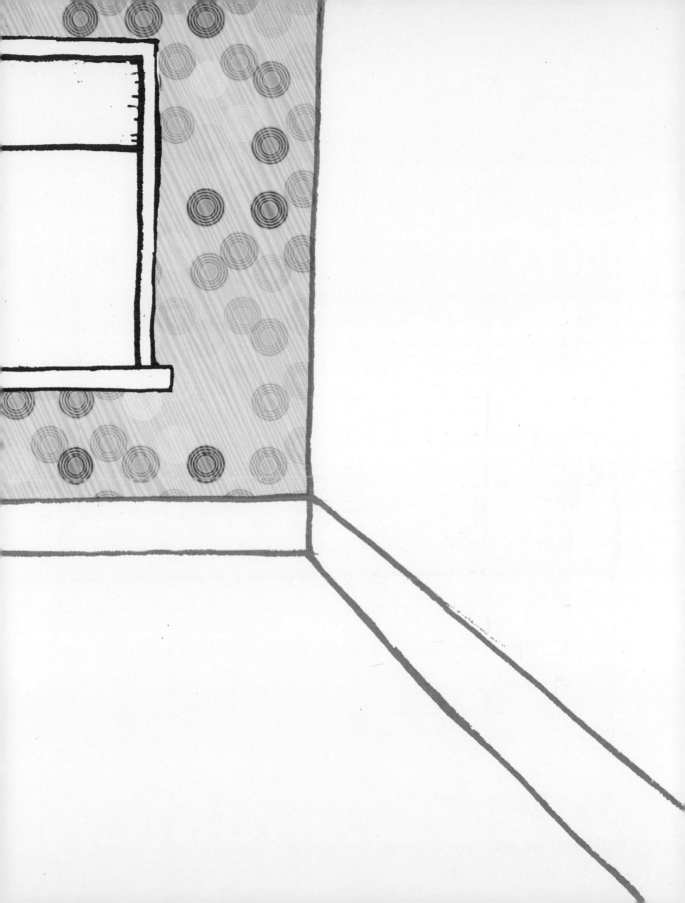

Fill these pages with different
animal footprints.

Fill this **seabed** with life.

Fill these jars with your favorite
candies and cookies.

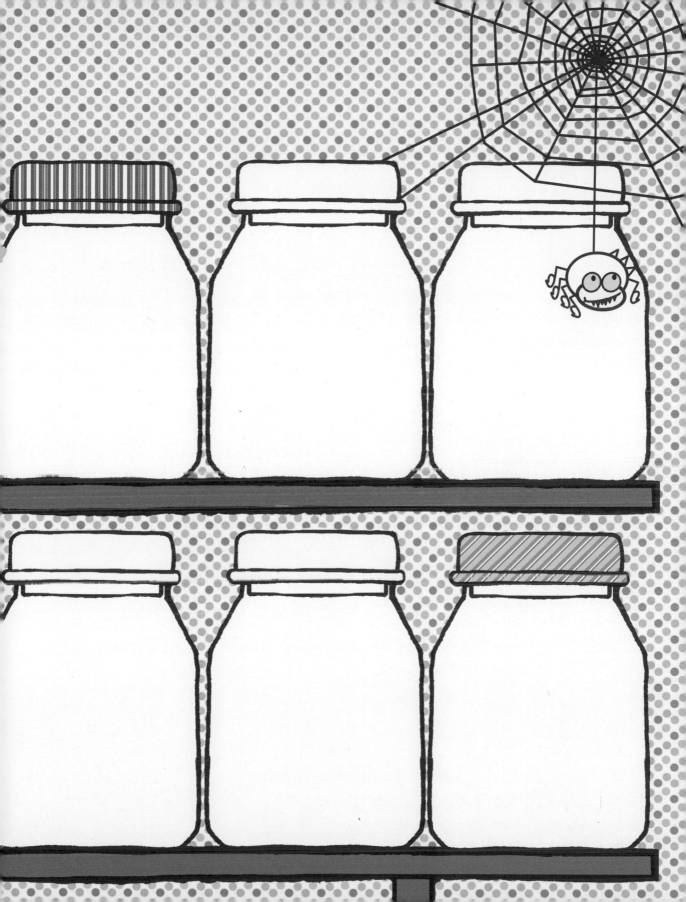

Draw our **galaxy**; the milky way.

Draw a panda, zebra, and penguin in primary colors.

**Fill this forest
scene with nocturnal
animals.**

Fill this page with diamonds.

Can you turn those diamonds into something alive?

Plant a **flower garden** on these pages.

Create your own **stained glass** windows.

Finish this cityscape.

Draw some **automobiles** on this street.

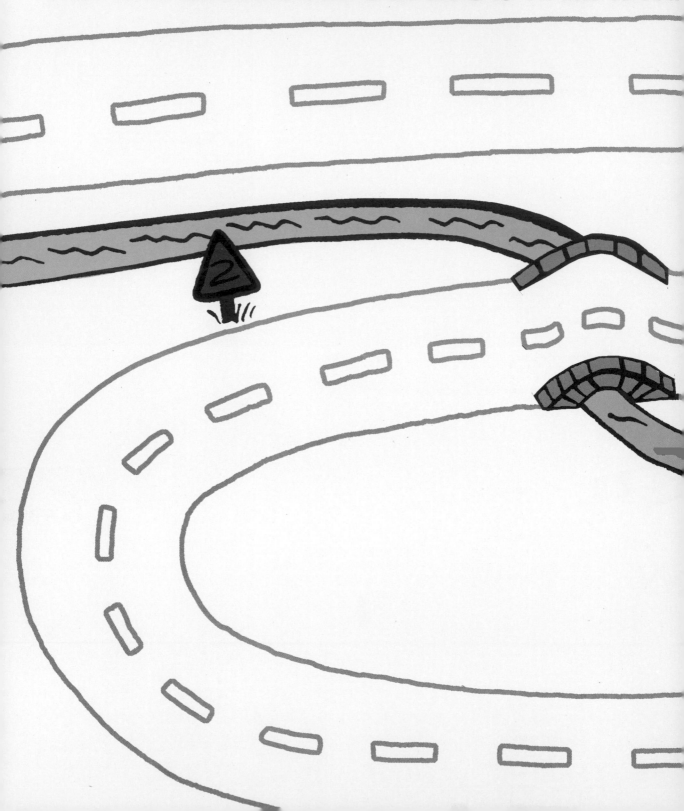

Finish the design on this rug.

Add personalities to the
people in this crowd.

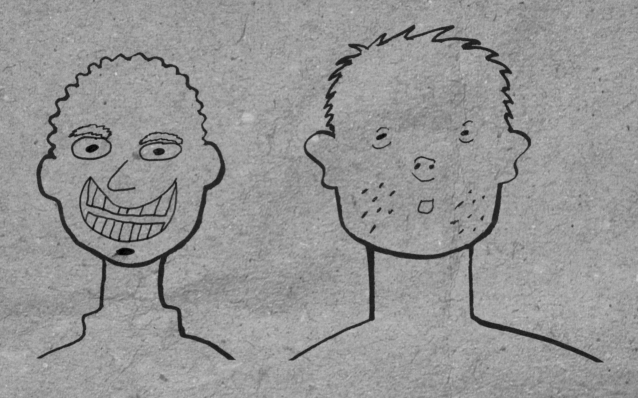

Fill this jar with
jelly beans.

Fill this page with stars.

Can you change those stars into patterns?

Fill the sky and trees with birds.

Color these pages.

Color these party hats.

Now design your own.

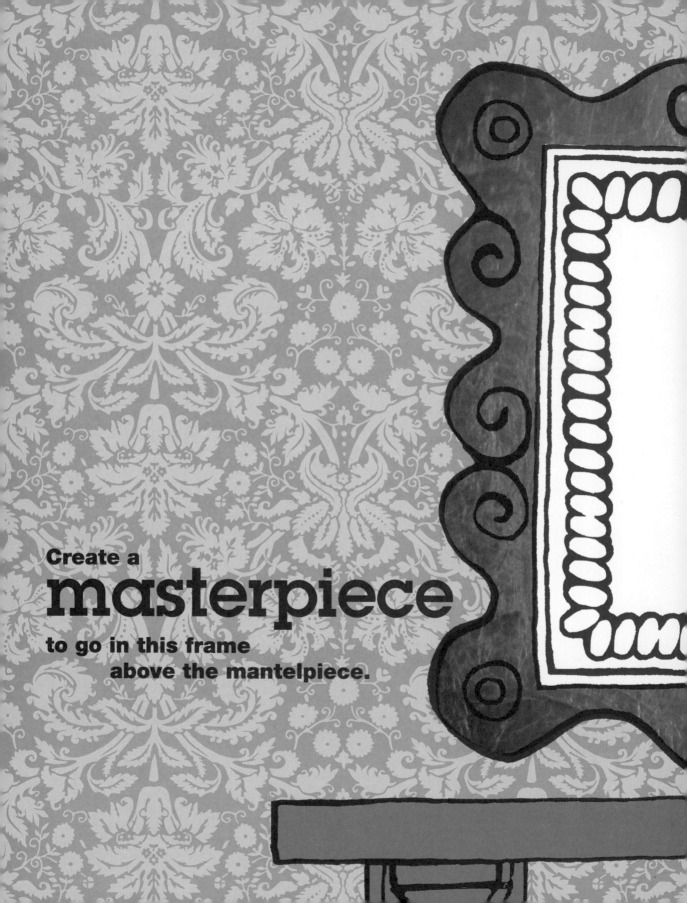

Create a
masterpiece
to go in this frame
above the mantelpiece.

Turn these shapes into **fish.**

Color

every other square.

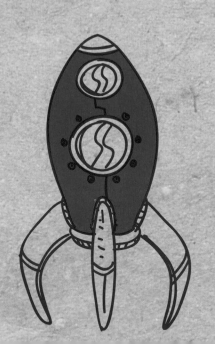

Design a beautiful
ball gown
for this girl.

Design an accompanying outfit for this boy.

Space for your art.

Doodle **cats** and **dogs.**

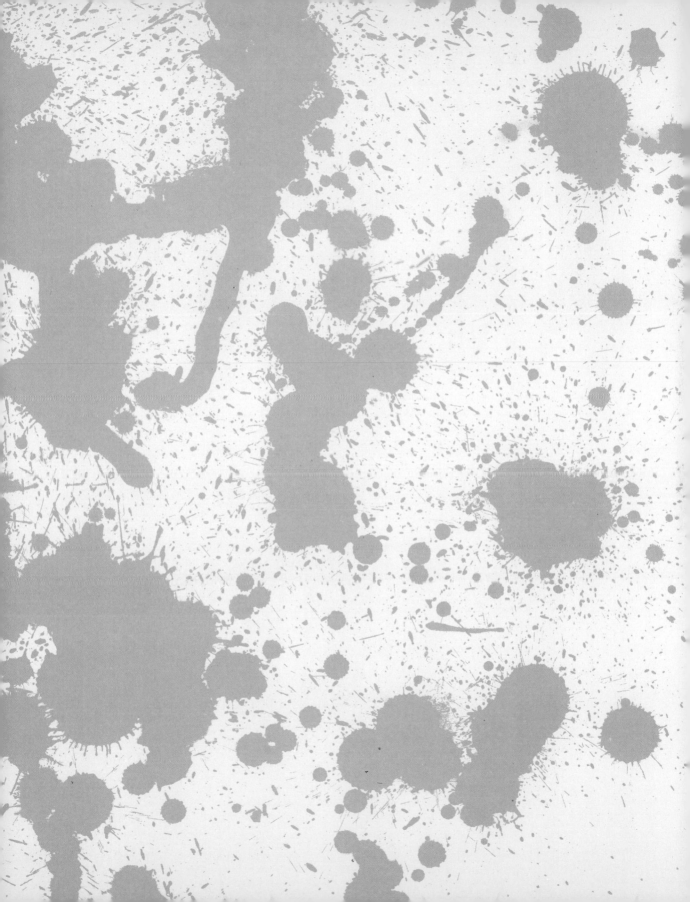

Draw **clothes** drying on this clothesline.

Draw what's above and below the sea level.

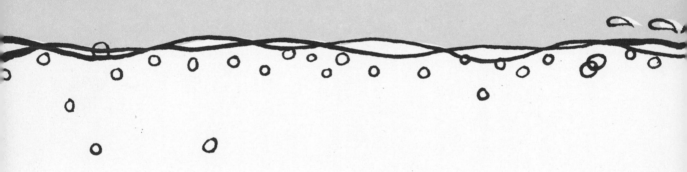

Fill these frames with
abstract art.

Fill this jar with
coins.

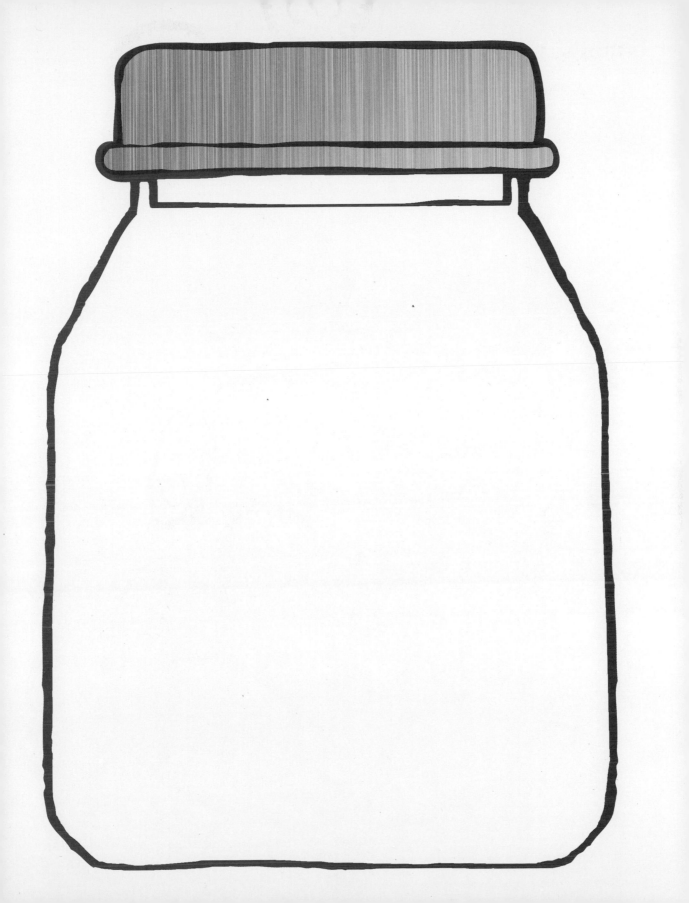

Draw this princess
a tower.

Fill these pages with

snowflakes.

Fill these pages with
fairies.

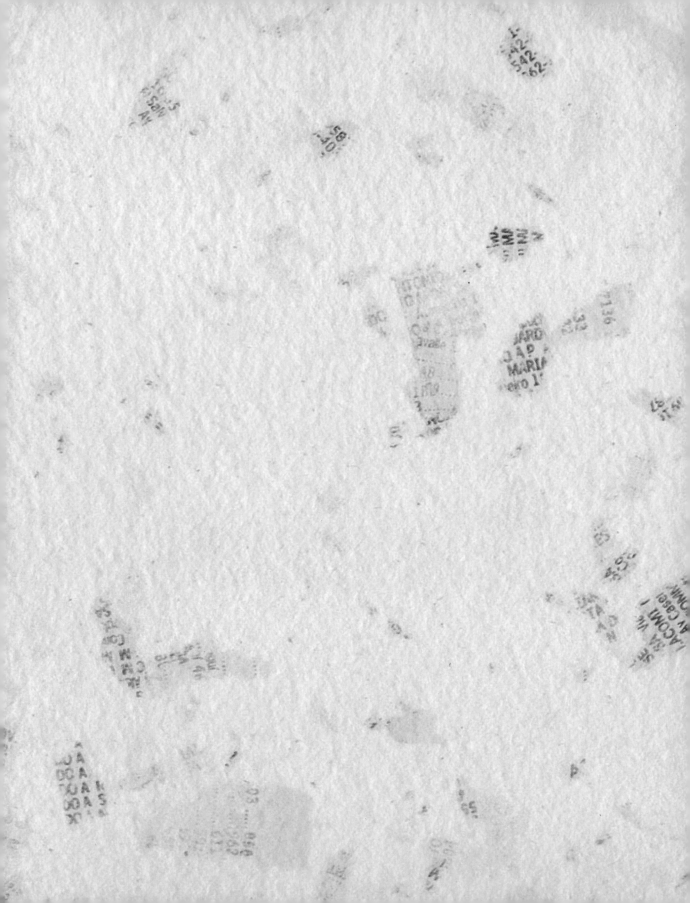

Fill these pages with
patterned hearts.

Add life to this
planet.

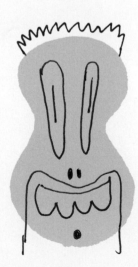

Make these shapes into different faces.

Draw the ingredients for your favorite meal.

Fill this plate with your favorite food.

Color these shoes.

Now **design** your own.

Design these pillows.

Draw the other half of this
teddy bear.

Add more vehicles to create a
traffic jam.

Design the **hot-air balloons** in this race.

Draw a **backyard**
that can be seen through these patio doors.

Doodle **frogs** and **flies.**

Give these flowers **petals.**